Also in the *Meet* . . . series

Look out for more *Meet* . . . books coming soon

Meet...

Nellie Melba

WRITTEN BY JANEEN BRIAN
ILLUSTRATED BY CLAIRE MURPHY

RANDOM HOUSE AUSTRALIA

To Sing Australia, for the joy of music – J.B.
For Edward and Amelie – C.M.

A Random House book
Published by Penguin Random House Australia Pty Ltd
Level 3, 100 Pacific Highway, North Sydney NSW 2060
www.penguin.com.au

First published by Random House Australia in 2016

Addresses for the Penguin Random House group of companies can be found at global.penguinrandomhouse.com/offices.

National Library of Australia
Cataloguing-in-Publication Entry

Creator: Brian, Janeen, author
Title: Meet . . . Nellie Melba / Janeen Brian; illustrated by Claire Murphy
ISBN: 9780143780298 (hardback)
Series: Meet; 11
Target Audience: For children
Subjects: Melba, Nellie, Dame, 1861–1931 – Juvenile literature
Sopranos (Singers) – Australia – Juvenile literature
Other Creators/Contributors: Murphy, Claire, illustrator
Dewey Number: 782.1092

Cover and internal design by Kirby Armstrong
Printed and bound in China by RR Donnelley

Dame Nellie Melba

was Australia's first classical music star. The beauty of her singing was celebrated around the globe. This is the story of how she rose to fame, and how she brought opera to Australians in the cities and the bush.

‘Nellie!’ David Mitchell snapped at his eldest daughter. ‘Stop that whistling! You sound like a tomboy.’

Dark-haired Nellie jutted her jaw. ‘Then I’ll hum.’

Nellie Porter Mitchell’s mother taught Nellie to sing and play the piano at their home in Richmond, Melbourne. Nellie *loved* music and she exercised her voice by humming.

In her late teens, Nellie took singing lessons from an Italian master. But her strict father said, 'You can sing for friends or at charity events, Nellie, but not on stage. It's not proper.'

Nellie had other ideas. She dreamed of becoming a world-famous soprano singer. If only she could hear the great opera stars of Europe, Britain or America. But there were no voice recordings and opera companies didn't visit distant Australia.

When Nellie was 20, her mother and a young sister died a few months apart. Full of grief, Nellie's father took a new job at a sugar plantation and moved the family to north Queensland.

Nellie married and had a son, George. Tropical rain drummed constantly on Nellie's small, iron-roofed house. The damp rotted her piano and she grew miserable. Her father said she should be content with having a home and family, but Nellie still had her dream. And a will of iron.

Nellie returned to Melbourne and her singing lessons. Her first public concert in Melbourne was a success. She was called the 'Australian nightingale' because of her beautiful silvery voice. But although Nellie was finding fame on stage, in private her marriage was unhappy and she had no money or freedom of her own.

BENGAL

When her father took a job in London, Nellie's eyes lit up. Perhaps this was her chance to sing overseas. Nellie and her family went too.

No one in England had heard of Nellie and she struggled to find teachers willing to train her. When she finally performed on stage, the applause was only polite.

Devastated, Nellie gave one last audition, for Madame Mathilde Marchesi in Paris. Mathilde was the leading opera teacher in Europe. When Mathilde stopped her mid-song, Nellie's heart sank.
She'd failed. But the teacher knew she had a star pupil. 'Nellie,' said Madame Marchesi, 'I will make something *extra*-ordinary of you.'

Under Madame Marchesi's guidance, Nellie stepped into the high-society world and saw her first opera. She chose a stage name, Melba, in honour of her hometown.

She studied hard, using her razor-sharp memory to learn the difficult songs. And, against the custom of the day, Nellie worked and cared for her son as a single mother, while her husband remained in England.

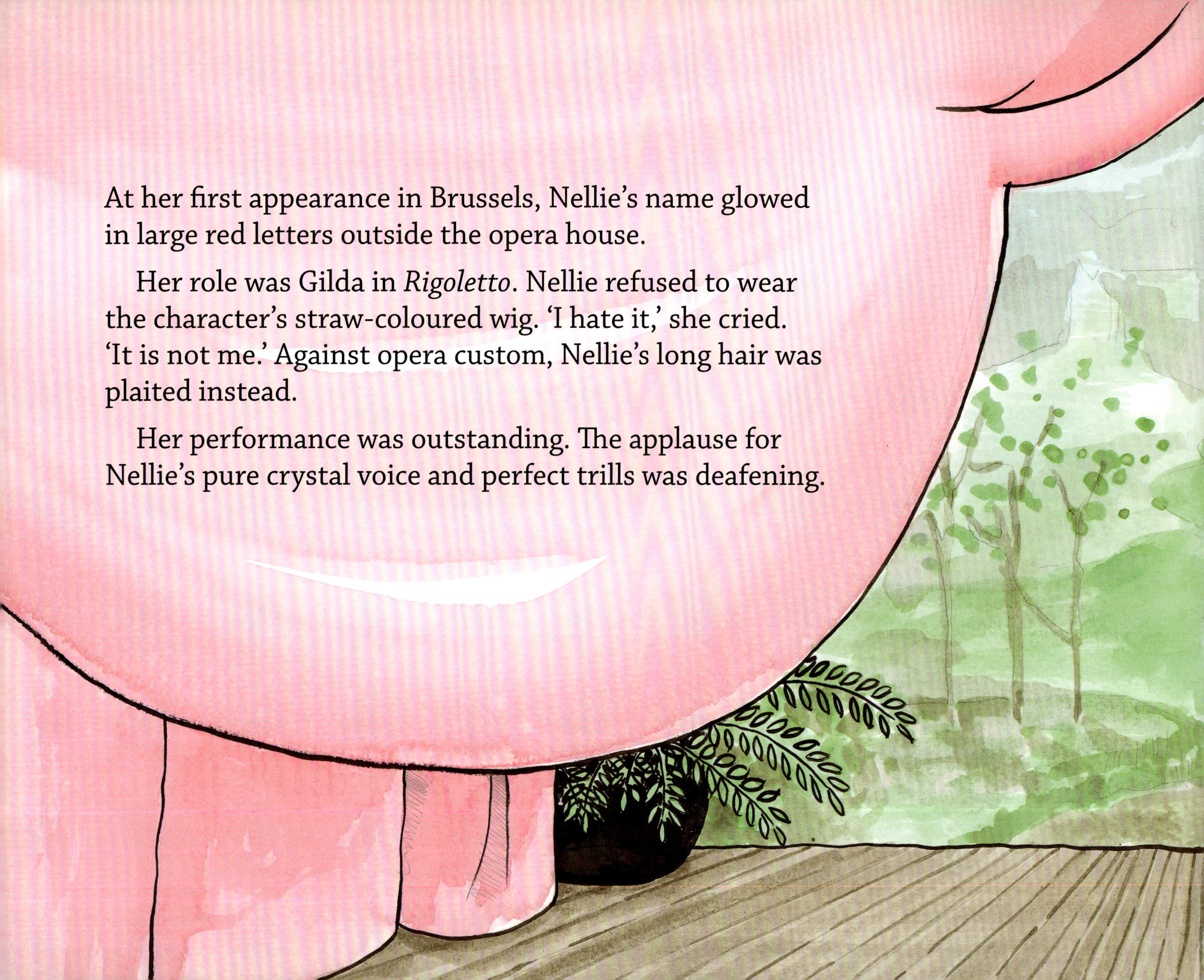

At her first appearance in Brussels, Nellie's name glowed in large red letters outside the opera house.

Her role was Gilda in *Rigoletto*. Nellie refused to wear the character's straw-coloured wig. 'I hate it,' she cried. 'It is not me.' Against opera custom, Nellie's long hair was plaited instead.

Her performance was outstanding. The applause for Nellie's pure crystal voice and perfect trills was deafening.

But it was different when she performed in England, at the famous Royal Opera House in Covent Garden. Another soprano had the leading role. And when Nellie sang Lucia, in *Lucia di Lammermoor*, the reviews focused on her acting.

‘I was there to sing!’ she cried. Disgruntled, Nellie left for Brussels.

A wealthy friend begged Nellie to return to Covent Garden and helped her get the roles she deserved. From then on, Nellie's performances received thunderous applause and her reputation grew and grew. She ruled Covent Garden for many years and sang in the major opera houses of Europe and the United States. Her voice was so splendid that kings, queens, tsars and emperors wanted to hear her sing.

But Nellie's heart remained in Australia.

Nellie was proud of her country at a time when the rest of the world rarely thought about it. In turn, Australians mobbed Nellie like royalty when she came home to perform.

She toured the cities and the outback alike. On one tour, Nellie insisted that everyone had the right to hear her sing, not just the wealthy, and so tickets were set at the same low price. Australians called her 'Our Melba' and 'Our Greatest Daughter'.

When World War I broke out, Nellie was in Australia. Travel to Europe was difficult and dangerous, and many of the great theatres were closed. Nellie turned her attention to raising money for war charities. She even auctioned flags at the end of her concerts. Nellie was made a Dame for her war-time fundraising.

In Melbourne, Nellie set up a music school so she could teach young Australian singers all she had learnt.

Towards the end of her career, Nellie sang at the opening of Canberra's first Parliament House.

'I must sing!' she once said, 'or I will die.' Through her talent and determination, Nellie Melba proved that a woman from far-away Australia could excel on the world's most exclusive stages. And she helped Australians learn and enjoy the music she so loved.

Timeline

1861 (19 May): Helen Porter Mitchell is born in Richmond, Melbourne.

1867: Six-year-old Helen, whose family nickname is Nellie, sings publicly for the first time at the Richmond Town Hall.

1875–80: Nellie attends the Presbyterian Ladies' College in Melbourne and later studies music with Italian opera singer Pietro Cecchi.

1881: Nellie's mother dies.

1882: Nellie's youngest sister dies. Her father decides a change is needed and moves the family to a sugarcane plantation in Mackay, Queensland.

1882: Nellie and Charles Armstrong, Irishman and horse trainer, marry in Brisbane.

1883: A son, George, is born.

1884: Nellie leaves Mackay, returns to singing lessons and gives her first professional concert at the Melbourne Town Hall.

1886: Nellie's father is invited to work in London. Nellie and her family accompany him.

1886: Travelling to Paris, Nellie studies with the famous opera teacher Mathilde Marchesi and changes her surname to Melba, in honour of her hometown, Melbourne.

1887: Aged 26, Nellie gives her first operatic performance as Gilda in Verdi's *Rigoletto* in Brussels. Her success earns her the nickname, 'Queen of Song'.

1889: Nellie returns to London to star at the Royal Opera House, Covent Garden.

1893: She gives her debut performance at the Metropolitan Opera House in New York.

1893: Famous French chef Georges-Auguste Escoffier creates the dessert Peach Melba in Nellie's honour. Four years later he creates Melba Toast.

1900: Nellie and Charles divorce.

1902–03: Returning home, Nellie's concert tour in Australia and then New Zealand is a triumphant success. Worldwide, Nellie is considered the most famous and talented soprano of her time.

1904: Back in London, Nellie makes the first of her 200 commercial recordings for gramophone. The technology was new at the time and Nellie was one of the first international stars to have performances recorded.

1909 (March): Travelling with two baby grand pianos, Nellie begins a tour that covers more than 16,000 kilometres and takes her to remote Australian outback towns.

1909 (November): Nellie buys a property at Coldstream, Lilydale, in Victoria, where Coombe Cottage will be built.

1911 (and 1924 and 1928): Nellie organises for the Melba-Williamson Opera Company to tour Australia.

1914: Because of her father's ill health, Nellie returns to Australia.

1914–18: She works tirelessly for the World War I war effort both in Australia and Northern America. For her work and fundraising, she is made a Dame Commander of the Order of the British Empire.

1915: Nellie begins a singing school at the Albert Street Conservatorium.

1916: Nellie's father dies.

1920: She becomes the first famous international artist to take part in direct radio broadcasts.

1922: Nellie sings at the Concerts for the People in Melbourne and Sydney, which offered affordable seats. The combined audiences number around 100,000.

1924: Nellie begins a series of farewell performances.

1925: *Melodies and Memories*, Nellie's autobiography, is published.

1926: Nellie gives her last performance in Covent Garden.

1927: She sings at the opening of Parliament House in Canberra. A month later, Nellie is made a Dame Grand Cross of the Order of the British Empire.

1928: Nellie gives her final Australian concerts.

1931 (23 February): Aged 69, Nellie dies in Sydney and is buried in Lilydale cemetery, Victoria. In her will she leaves £8000 to the Conservatorium of Music, Melbourne, 'in the hope that another Melba may arise'. This bequest is now called the Melba Opera Trust.

1996: Nellie is featured on the new $100 banknote, in recognition of her contribution to Australian society.